TWISTED

THE GIRL WHO GREW NASTY THINGS

Wil Mara

An imprint of Enslow Publishing

WEST **44** BOOKS™

THE VIDEOMANIAC   WHERE DID MY FAMILY GO?
HOUSE OF A MILLION ROOMS   THE GIRL WHO GREW NASTY THINGS
THE TIME TRAP

Please visit our website, www.west44books.com. For a free color catalog of all our high-quality books, call toll free 1-800-542-2595 or fax 1-877-542-2596.

Cataloging-in-Publication Data

Names: Mara, Wil.
Title: The girl who grew nasty things / Wil Mara.
Description: New York : West 44, 2020. | Series: Twisted
Identifiers: ISBN 9781538383667 (pbk.) | ISBN 9781538383612 (library bound) |
  ISBN 9781538383568 (ebook)
Subjects: LCSH: Plants--Juvenile fiction. | Growth (Plants)--Juvenile fiction. |
  Supernatural--Juvenile fiction.
Classification: LCC PZ7.M373 Gi 2020 | DDC [F]--dc23

Published in 2020 by
Enslow Publishing LLC
101 West 23rd Street, Suite #240
New York, NY 10011

Editor: Caitie McAneney
Designer: Rachel Rising
Interior Layout: Seth Hughes

Photo Credits: Cover (background) Georgios Kritsotakis/Shutterstock.com; Cover (insert) Jan Dempers/EyeEm/Getty Images; Back Cover (background) STILLFX/Shutterstock.com.

Printed in the United States of America

CPSIA compliance information: Batch #CS18W44: For further information contact
Enslow Publishing LLC, New York, New York at 1-800-542-2595.

To Debi and Madonna—thanks for all the great ideas

Maddie Dragonette sat by herself in a quiet corner of the school cafeteria. She sat at this same table every day. It was a small table with just one chair. It was used sometimes by the cafeteria's workers. Someone might sit and wrap sets of silverware into fresh napkins. Or write out the menu that would go on the school bulletin board. But during lunch period, the table was left open for Maddie. This wasn't an official rule or anything. It was just kind of understood.

Maddie sat by herself because she wanted to. She couldn't stand her classmates. For that matter, she really couldn't stand *anyone*. Other people made her angry. In fact, whenever she thought about them, she didn't even use the word "other." She just used the word "people," like she wasn't a person herself. And that's because, deep down, she *didn't* think of herself as a person. She wasn't sure what she was exactly. But she was absolutely certain that she wasn't one of *them*. She was better.

People made her angry. She didn't like the way they walked. She didn't like the way they talked. She didn't like their clothes, their shoes, or their hair. She didn't like that some girls played on the school's softball team. She hated softball. And because she hated it, she thought everyone else should hate it, too. And anyone who didn't hate it—well, she hated them for *not* hating it.

She hated social studies, too. So she hated everyone who liked it. One of the boys

in her social studies class was named Jordan.
He was the smartest kid in the school. Maddie
really hated that. She hated all the kids who
were smart. And that's because, deep down, she
knew she really wasn't too bright. She would
never be as smart as Jordan. Or Billy Palmer.
Or Allie Moskowitz. Or any of the smart kids.
So she hated them, and that took care of that.

She had decided long ago that hating
people was the answer to all of her problems.

Maddie unpacked her lunch from the
brown paper bag. Then she unwrapped her
sandwich and took a bite. It was chicken with
lettuce, tomato, and mayo. As she chewed, she
looked at the sandwich carefully. Her mother
had made it that morning. The chicken looked

good. All white meat, shredded into little pieces. There was the right amount of mayo. And the lettuce was nice and crisp.

But the tomato…that was a problem.

There was a spot in the middle where it was orange instead of red. And it was hard, too. Maddie didn't like that one bit. She liked having the best of everything. She felt she deserved it. And this wasn't the best sandwich it could have been. So she made a note in her mind. She was going to talk to her mother about the tomato when she got home. She might even do more than talk. She might have to yell a little. That was okay, though. Yelling at people was one thing Maddie Dragonette did love. It made her feel great.

She took another bite and looked around the cafeteria. It was really crowded at the moment. Some of the other kids were classmates of hers. They paid no attention to her. They never did. It was like she wasn't even there. They all talked and laughed and had a good time. Something about this really bothered her. Seeing people happy…it just *bothered* her.

She made a point of looking at Olivia Robinson. Olivia was sitting with three other friends. They looked like they were having the greatest day ever. Maddie knew all about Olivia. She was a straight-A student. She played field hockey, basketball, and—so gross—softball. She was a cheerleader. She had beautiful golden hair. She never said a bad word about anyone. And she was always cheerful. Sometimes Olivia sat and talked to people who *weren't* feeling cheerful. She was the type of person who really cared about others. Everyone loved her, and Maddie *really* hated that. She hated people who everyone else loved.

But none of that was important to Maddie right now. The important thing was what Olivia was holding. It was a beautiful necklace. It had a gold chain and a flower-shaped pendant. Maddie did like flowers. That's because she liked to grow things. Back home, she grew lots of things. Some were pretty. Some were not. A few were downright nasty. But that was okay. Nasty things could be useful sometimes.

Olivia held up the necklace so her friends could see it. Maddie had heard her talking about it in gym class. It was a gift from her aunt. Olivia had helped her clean out her basement last weekend. She also had the necklace's box, which had a little bow on top.

Maddie pretended she wasn't watching Olivia. But she was, very carefully. She was waiting, and she was getting tired of it. Olivia had her own sandwich out. She had put it on the table and unwrapped it. But she hadn't taken a bite yet. All she was doing was yapping about her precious necklace.

Olivia set it back in its box. Then she picked up the sandwich. She was about to take a bite. But she started laughing instead. One of her friends had said something funny. Maddie couldn't hear what it was, and she really didn't care.

Come on...she thought. *Come ON*...

Finally, Olivia took a bite. It was a big one. She chewed it around for a moment. It made her cheeks bulge, first on one side and then the other. Then she swallowed it. Maddie got a warm feeling in her own stomach. She had to fight back a smile.

Olivia started laughing again. Then

everything changed. Her eyes grew wide, and her face began turning red. She started coughing. First only a little, then a lot. Her hands went to her throat. She tried to say something, but Maddie couldn't hear it. Now she looked really scared. All her friends did, too.

The one sitting next to her started rubbing her back. She asked Olivia what was wrong. Olivia said something about her sandwich being hot. Not *hot* hot, she said, but spicy hot. Other people began to notice what was happening. They came over to see. Then one of the women who worked in the cafeteria appeared. The name on her tag read "Ms. Patterson."

Ms. Patterson looked more scared than even Olivia did. By this time, Olivia was looking a little better. She had taken a few sips from her water bottle. But her face was still red. It was kind of shiny, too. She was so scared that she started sweating.

Ms. Patterson asked Olivia if she was okay. Olivia said her throat was still burning really bad. Ms. Patterson said she should go to the nurse. Olivia nodded and got up. Ms. Patterson led her away. Her friends all went along.

Just as they got to the door, however, one of Olivia's friends stopped. This was Hannah Kim. Thin, athletic, dark hair, very pretty. She wasn't in any of Maddie's classes this year. Maddie was happy about that. Hannah was the kind of girl who raised her hand at every question. And she always got the answers right. Maddie often wished terrible things would happen to her.

Hannah came back to the table to get

everyone's stuff. Then she noticed the box with the necklace was gone. She looked around for it, but it was nowhere in sight. She asked if anyone saw what happened to it. No one had.

Hannah looked very upset now. Maddie liked that.

A lot.

Maddie lay on her bed a few hours later. Her room was kind of like the rooms of other kids. There were a few stuffed animals on the dresser, and some posters on the walls. A big TV was tucked in one corner. Next to that was a shelf loaded with books. The closet had a pair of sliding doors. One door was open, and dirty clothes were piled on the floor inside.

What made the room different, though, were all the plants and flowers. They were everywhere. There were two in small pots on the dresser. Three others were in much bigger pots on the floor. And there was a cactus on Maddie's nightstand. It looked like a fuzzy cucumber half buried in the dirt. But most of them were in the windows. Maddie didn't have normal windows. Instead, they were like big glass boxes that stuck out from the house. Each one had three shelves. Some had plants that were long and flowing, almost like hair. Others were tall and spiky. Some were green, others were brown or red or pink. Some had big, floppy leaves. Others had very tiny leaves.

Maddie didn't think of them as plants or flowers or whatever. She thought of them kind of like children. *Her* children. She loved looking at them and taking care of them. She also loved talking to them. She imagined that they talked back to her, too. And they always said what she wanted to hear. They said what she wanted, and they *did* what she wanted. That's what she liked best about them. Whatever she wanted them to do, they did it. She was the boss here. Always.

She reached over and got her backpack from the floor. It was pretty heavy because of all the schoolbooks. She unzipped it and dug around inside. Then she pulled out a box. It had a small red bow on top. She opened the box and took out Olivia's necklace. She lay back again and held it high. It swung back and forth a little. The flower pendant had a perfect sparkle to it.

All mine, she thought with a smile. Then she remembered how upset Hannah had been when she came back to the table and couldn't find the box. Maddie's smile grew even bigger. And Hannah hadn't been half as upset as Olivia when she found out what happened. Olivia had been crying, and all her friends tried to comfort her. Maddie saw them walking through the hall. Tears were running down

Olivia's face, and everyone was around her. They were treating her like she was a celebrity or something. Maddie didn't say anything. But she couldn't help standing there and watching. Something about seeing Olivia cry made her feel great.

Tough luck, Olivia, Maddie told herself. *I wanted it.* She had stolen things from other kids before. And this is what she always thought afterward. If she wanted something, that was a good enough reason to take it. Was it unfair? Was it mean? Maybe. *But that's their problem,* Maddie always believed. *They'll get over it.*

The door to her room opened slowly. Then Maddie's mom stuck her head in. She looked kind of like Maddie. Same reddish hair, same freckles. But she was much older. And she *seemed* even older than she was. There were dark half-moons under her eyes. Her skin kind of sagged a bit. And her hair was starting to go gray in some places. She certainly wasn't old enough for gray hair—yet there it was.

"Hey, sweetie," her mom said. Her voice was very soft and quiet. "How was school today?"

Maddie never stopped looking at the necklace. "Fine," she replied.

"How did your math test go?"

"Good," Maddie told her. She knew what her mom really wanted to know. She wanted to know if Maddie got a good grade on the test. She had gotten a C. She knew this because Mr. Oldham had graded the tests right away. But she didn't feel like talking about it. Besides, her mom could always go online and find out. The school had a site now where parents could follow their kids' grades. But her mom had a strange fear of computers. She had a strange fear of a lot of things. And Maddie used it against her.

"Do you know if you got a—"

"The sandwich was wrong," Maddie said.

"What, honey?"

"The chicken sandwich. It wasn't right."

"What…what was wrong about it?"

"The tomato wasn't ripe. It was hard in the middle. It was orange, too. That means it wasn't ripe. It was disgusting. I had to take it off and throw it away. Then I had to eat the sandwich without it. I *hate* chicken sandwiches without tomatoes."

"Oh, Maddie, I'm so sorry. If you want, I could make you another one right n—"

"I don't want one now," Maddie replied. "I wanted one at lunch."

"I was sure I used a good tomato when I made—"

"You didn't. You used a bad tomato. You used one from your garden, not from mine." Maddie looked to her at last. "Is that right? You used one from *your* garden?"

Her mom froze, her eyes wide. "Yes," she said, nodding very slowly.

"I told you never to do that. You don't know anything about gardening."

"That's not true."

"You couldn't grow something right if your life depended on it."

"Now, Maddie, that's no way to talk to your mother."

Maddie's smile from before had disappeared. Now it was back.

"You want to argue with me about growing things?"

Now her mom looked positively terrified.

"No, no...I'm sorry I brought it up."

Maddie laughed just a little. Then she went back to admiring the necklace.

"What…what's that you have there?" her mom asked.

"I found it on the playground," Maddie replied. She had some idea of what her mom wanted to say next. Something like, *Well, why don't you bring it to the office? Or the lost and found?* Her mom was a big believer in Doing The Right Thing.

Maddie found this incredibly annoying. Doing the right thing was for suckers, she thought. It didn't get you anything. Maybe people liked you more. But Maddie didn't care if anyone liked her. She just wanted people to be afraid of her. Maddie knew her mom was afraid of her. She loved this. Like right now, for example. There was just something great about seeing her standing there, scared half to death.

"You…you found it on the playground?" her mom asked.

"Yeah," Maddie replied. She knew more questions would follow. So she faked a big yawn. Then she said, "I'm feeling a little tired, so I want to take a nap. Could you close the door, please?"

Her mom hung there for a moment, saying nothing. She looked more frightened than ever. Then she did as Maddie asked.

Maddie enjoyed listening to her footsteps as she walked away.

Maddie and her mom lived in a very big house. It used to belong to her mom's parents. Then they died and Maddie's mom got it. Maddie liked the house very much. She dreamed of having it all to herself one day. She once heard her mom on the phone talking to a friend. She told the friend she thought about giving the house to some charity organization or something.

Maddie got very angry about this. She went and had a talk with her mom. She made her mom more frightened than she'd ever been before. Then her mom promised to give Maddie the house instead. Maddie was very happy after that. She could always get her mom to do what she wanted. All she had to do was scare her enough.

There were two gardens outside. One was by the east side of the house, the other by the west side. The house also had a tall fence around it. That meant no one else could see the gardens.

Maddie's mom's garden was on the west side. It was very tiny. It didn't get enough sunlight. And the dirt was always dry. But Maddie's garden was amazing. It was much bigger. It got lots of sunlight. And the dirt was nice and soft. Maddie made sure to water everything on days when it didn't rain.

She had rows of fruits and vegetables. Her favorite fruits were strawberries, raspberries, blueberries, and currants. Her favorite vegetables were green beans, yellow beans, peppers, and, of course, tomatoes. She always ate the things that she grew. Sometimes her mom ate from Maddie's garden, too. But if Maddie was mad at her, she wouldn't let her.

At the far end of Maddie's garden was a greenhouse. It looked like a big shed. But it wasn't made of wood. Instead, everything— the walls, the roof, the door—was made of glass. It looked like it had been built using nothing but windows. And it once belonged to Maddie's grandmother, who died many years ago.

There were long tables inside. They were covered with more plants and flowers. Hundreds, in fact. And the shelves hanging above the tables had even more. Maddie also kept all of her gardening stuff in here. There were little shovels and rakes. There were bags of dirt. And there were jars of plant food. A pair of overalls hung from a hook by the door. Maddie always put these on before she did any work. There was also a big hat to protect her face from the sun. And there were several pairs of gloves. Most important of all, though, was the book. It was big like a notebook. But it had a hard leather cover. Three words were printed on the front:

My
Gardening
Secrets

Maddie loved this book more than anything in the world.

There was a waist-high fence at the other end of Maddie's garden. And it had a gate on one side. Maddie opened the gate, then checked over all the fruits and vegetables. She picked off the bad ones and threw them into a pile. They would rot there, and Maddie knew that was good. It would put vitamins and minerals back into the ground. That would help everything else grow better.

Then she went into the greenhouse. It was very hot inside, and it smelled like fresh dirt. Maddie loved being in here. She got a pair of clippers. These looked kind of like scissors. Then she went to each plant and began snipping off all the dead leaves and stems.

She smiled when she got to one plant in particular. It was actually very ugly. The leaves were all twisted and uneven. They were a weird mix of red and green. Some grew straight up. Others sagged over the side.

She ran her fingers gently over the leaves. Like she was petting a cat or dog.

"You did good," she said to it. Then she pointed to the flower pendant, which hung from the gold chain around her neck. "See this? Without you, I wouldn't have it."

It had been so easy and so simple. She knew that those ugly leaves were poisonous to people. Not enough to kill anyone. But it certainly would make them feel pretty bad for awhile. So she clipped a few off. Then she ground them up into very tiny bits. The next day in homeroom, she took Olivia's lunch bag when she wasn't looking. She sprinkled the bits into her sandwich. After that, all Maddie had to do was wait.

She reached under the table and got a spray bottle. Then she pumped a few shots into the ugly plant's dirt.

"A little food, just for you. My way of saying thank you."

A few minutes later she went over to the book. She opened it carefully. It was very old. Some of the pages were starting to brown around the edges. There were lines on each page just like in a normal notebook. And there was lots of writing. It was very neat and beautiful. The ink had begun to turn brown.

At the top of the first page, in capital letters, it said:

GERANIUMS

And just under that:

CAN BE USED TO MAKE TEA. ALSO
GOOD FOR HEADACHES.

Then there were all sorts of tips on how
to care for them. One said:

NEED LOTS OF SUNLIGHT.

Another said:

SOIL SHOULD BE KEPT MOIST.

A third said:

DON'T PLANT THEM TOO
CLOSE TOGETHER.

The handwriting was her grandmother's. Maddie had never known her. In fact, this book was all Maddie had of her. There weren't any pictures of her, and her mom wouldn't talk about her. Maddie had heard that she died very young. But she couldn't find out what happened. It was all very mysterious.

Then she found this book. She had been digging through some boxes while looking for string. She needed to tie up a few tomato plants that were leaning over. She didn't find the string, but the book was at the bottom of one of the boxes.

She asked her mom about it. The moment her mom saw it, she got all weird. Kind of angry and frightened at the same time. She told Maddie to give it to her, but Maddie wouldn't. Then they got into a big argument about it. Maddie got her way in the end like always. And she got her mom to admit that the book had, in fact, belonged to her grandmother.

Maddie was amazed her grandmother had been so interested in gardening. Maddie always loved to garden, so that was really cool. She wished her grandmother was still alive so they could talk about it. But at least she had the book.

She read every page with great interest. And as she went along, she began to notice some unusual things. Her grandmother's comments on what certain plants and flowers could do, for example. Early in the book they were very simple. One might say:

HELPS TO CLEAN WINDOWS.

Another might say:

MAKES A NICE SMELL WHEN YOU
BURN THE LEAVES.

But then Maddie saw one that said:

WILL CAUSE SOMEONE TO SNEEZE
OVER AND OVER.

And another that said:

WILL GIVE SOMEONE A BAD RASH.

And there was one that read:

WILL MAKE SOMEONE VERY DIZZY.

By the time Maddie reached the end of
the book, she found some stuff that even scared

her.

There was something else strange, too. She noticed that her grandmother's handwriting changed as the book went along. At the beginning, it was very neat. At the end, however, it was all shaky. Like she had been writing in a car that was going down a bumpy road or something. Maddie had no idea what that was all about. And she didn't really care, either. She only cared that the book had helped her do all sorts of nasty things.

And it'll help me do many more, she thought with a smile. *I'm sure of that.*

Maddie took her time walking through the halls in school the next day. There was lots of talk about The Mystery of Olivia's Necklace. Everyone seemed to have a different idea about what happened. But none of those ideas had anything to do with Maddie. That meant she'd gotten away with it. That was a great feeling. She loved being the only one who knew the truth. She also heard that Olivia was still very upset. That felt great, too.

She passed by the cafeteria and turned right. This hallway led to many different places. One door was for the art room. Another was for the science lab. And there were two doors that stood together at the far end. These were for the auditorium. Maddie saw that there was a small poster on one of them. She went down to take a look at it. At the top was one word in big letters—

AUDITIONS

She knew what this meant. The school was going to have a play, and they needed kids to act in it. The auditions would help them decide who the actors would be. It was like trying out for the baseball team.

Maddie liked the idea of acting. She always thought she'd be good at it. She knew she was good at lying to people. And pretending she was feeling things that she really wasn't. She was always able to make someone think she was happy or sad or whatever. She was also good at pretending she was interested in things. This was very useful for some of her classes.

Maddie also liked the idea of acting because she'd be on stage. That meant everyone would be looking at her. And when she did a great job, they'd all clap and cheer. She liked that very much. People *should* clap and cheer for her. She was so much better than them, after all. She deserved to be adored.

The name of the play was *The Demon Child*. It was about a girl named Ruby whose parents had always given her anything she wanted. Then her parents split up. Because of this, they weren't able to give her as much as before. That made her incredibly angry. And when she got angry, she did all sorts of mean and terrible things. She became evil. The school always did a play of some scary story each year around Halloween. The kids in her class just loved to *pretend* to be scary. *Cute*, Maddie thought.

Maddie always liked the school's Halloween plays. But the characters in the past didn't seem all that scary to her. Ruby, however, was different. Maddie thought she could definitely play the part.

In fact, she thought she'd be perfect as Ruby. There was something about the role that just seemed *right* to Maddie. Her own parents had split up a long time ago. She'd heard that her father just left one day. She had tried to contact him a few times since then. But he wanted nothing to do with her. So she knew what it felt like to be angry about this. Ruby's anger was *her* anger.

She looked back at the poster. It said there were other roles that needed to be filled.

There were Ruby's parents, and some of her friends. There were a few other, smaller parts, too. But Maddie wasn't interested in any of those. *Only Ruby herself,* she thought. *Because I'm going to be the star of the show.*

Printed at the very bottom of the poster was:

AUDITIONS WILL START TODAY AT 3:15

"I'll be there," she said.

Maddie walked into the auditorium at exactly 3:15. It had rows and rows of seats. And at the front was the stage. There were lights hanging over it, way up high. Something stirred deep inside Maddie when she saw these. The idea of standing under them was so exciting. The lights shining down on her…hundreds of people in the audience…watching her…listening to every word she said. And then, when the play was over, they would all clap and cheer.

I can't wait, she thought.

There were a lot of other kids there, both boys and girls. Ms. Klein was there, too. She was the drama teacher. She was an older woman, with a cloud of silver hair. She also wore glasses with a chain that hung around the back of her neck. And she seemed to have plenty of energy for someone her age.

She was standing on the stage, trying to get things under control.

"Everyone who is trying out for the part of Ruby should go over *there*!" she said. Then she pointed to a group of seats by the windows. "We'll take care of the other parts later. But first, we need to find out who'll be our Ruby!"

Maddie walked down the aisle and sat toward the back of this group. There were three other girls, all of whom she knew. She had no idea if any of them knew how to act. *It doesn't matter though*, she thought. *Because I AM Ruby Slaughter.*

Ms. Klein walked down the little flight of stairs at one side of the stage. Then she came over and began handing out copies of a sheet of paper.

"Okay," she said. "This is what you'll be reading when you try out for the part. It's a talk between Ruby and her mother."

The girl in front of Maddie took her copy, then handed the last one back.

"We'll have the auditions right up on the

stage," Ms. Klein said. "I will read the mom parts. And each of you will take a turn reading Ruby's part. Who wants to go first?"

Every hand went up except Maddie's. She had already decided to wait until the others had gone. She wanted to see how they did first.

Someone tapped her on the shoulder. She jumped a little because she wasn't expecting it. When she turned around, she found Connor Anderson sitting there with a pleasant smile on his face. Connor was in a few of her classes. She had never paid much attention to him, however. He was cute enough, with blond hair and green eyes. He always had a neat and tidy look about him. He kept every one of those blond hairs perfectly combed. And his clothes were never wrinkled.

"Hi, Maddie," he said in a friendly voice.

"Hi. What do you want?"

"You're trying out for the part of Ruby?"

"Yes."

"That's so cool. I didn't know you liked to act."

Maddie shrugged. "It's okay." She thought being the star of the school play was a lot more than okay. But she wasn't about to tell Connor about any of that.

"I'm trying out for the part of Ruby's dad," he told her.

"Whoop-de-doo for you," she replied. She knew this was a snotty thing to say. But that was what she wanted. She hoped Connor would take the hint and go away.

But he didn't—and that struck Maddie as very weird. Any time Maddie wanted someone to disappear, she'd say something snotty to them. She might get yelled at or whatever. But then the other person would finally leave.

Connor didn't leave, however. In fact, he just kept staring at her with that little smile. It wasn't a stupid kind of smile. Maddie knew Connor wasn't stupid. He was one of the smartest kids in their grade, in fact. And it wasn't a big, toothy smile. Like he was so excited that he could barely control himself. Maddie finally decided it was a very *adult* smile. It was calm, steady, and real. It was like Connor was a grown-up in a kid's body.

Then Maddie realized the truth, much to her horror...

He LIKES me.

Yes, that was it. No doubt about it. And it wasn't some goofy schoolboy crush, either. Maddie could sense that he *really* liked her. That's why his little grown-up smile didn't shrink when she said what she said. Because his liking for her was stronger than that.

And she had no idea what to do about it.

"I hope you get the part," he went on. "It would be fun up there together, wouldn't it?"

"Sure," Maddie replied. Then she held up the sheet Ms. Klein had handed out. "But I have to study these lines now, okay?"

"Oh, sure," Connor said, nodding. "Of course. Okay, good luck, Maddie!"

Then he was gone. Maddie watched him head back to the seats on the other side of the auditorium. There had to be at least fifty more kids over there. They were all waiting for their chance to audition for one of the other parts.

When Connor sat down, he looked back over at her. Then he gave her the thumbs-up sign. She didn't know what to do in return. So she did nothing.

About twenty minutes later, Ms. Klein called her name.

Five minutes after that, one thing was very clear—Maddie Dragonette was *not* an actress. And every person in the auditorium knew it.

Everyone, that is, except Maddie.

A few days went by. Maddie kept checking the doors to the auditorium. The little sheet about the auditions was still there on the first day. It was gone on the second. The doors were still bare on the third. Then she came in early on the fourth day, and a new sheet had been taped up.

At the top, it said:

THE FOLLOWING STUDENTS WILL BE PLAYING THE FOLLOWING ROLES IN *THE DEMON CHILD*

Beneath that was a list. And the very first line read—

`Ruby Slaughter: Christie Walker`

Maddie felt everything in her body stop. Her heart wasn't beating, her lungs weren't breathing. In fact, it felt like everything in the universe had come to a halt.

No…impossible, she told herself. *This is IMPOSSIBLE.*

A storm of emotions swirled up inside her. Disbelief, confusion, embarrassment… but most of all, anger. It was the emotion she knew better than any other. She felt it about a hundred times every day. It was like there was a volcano inside her. And the lava was always bubbling just below the surface, waiting to blow.

She had watched Christie Walker's

audition, and Christie *stunk*. Maddie believed she had been ten times better. No—a hundred times better.

I was incredible, she thought. *INCREDI*—

"Oh, Maddie," someone said. "I'm so sorry."

When she spun around, she found Connor there again. Every hair in place. His clothes looking like they'd been ironed ten minutes ago. And that smile, as annoying as ever.

"What?" she asked.

"I said I'm so sorry you didn't get the part of Ruby. It would have been fun to be in the play with you."

She could tell that he really meant it. For some reason that made it all the more irritating.

"Well, I didn't," she said. "Even though I was the best one."

Something passed over Connor's face when she said this. She saw it for just a moment, then it was gone. What had it been? Uncertainty? Doubt? *Pity*?!

Then it came to her—*He doesn't think I was that good.*

"There's going to be another play in the spring," he went on cheerfully. "That's how Ms. Klein does it. She has one in the fall—this year it's *The Demon Child*, obviously—and one in the spring. I try to be in all of them. I love to act."

Maddie looked back at the sheet. Sure enough, about halfway down, it said—

```
Ruby's Father: Connor Anderson
```

"Whoop-de-doo for you," she said again.

"You should audition for the one in the spring," he replied. Just like before, her snottiness didn't seem to bother him one bit. "I think it's going to be *House of a Million Rooms*. Either that or *The Time Trap*. The first one is the story of—"

"Yeah, whatever," Maddie said. Then she turned and began walking away.

"I can help you, Maddie!" Connor called out. "I've taken some acting lessons! I'll be happy to show you what I've learned!"

Maddie stopped. The first idea she had was to turn around and snap at him. Say something like, *I don't need any of your acting lessons!* Then she'd add something else. Maybe, *And stop talking to me! I'm not interested in you!*

But then she thought a little more. And she realized it would be dumb to say any of those things. *Because he can help me*, she thought. *Not with my acting—my acting is great. But with getting the part of Ruby.* She knew she could still do it. In fact, a whole plan came together very quickly in her head. She saw everything that she needed to do.

Yes—I can still be Ruby…

I know exactly how…

And Connor Anderson is going to help me.

She turned back around. Then she smiled at him. Connor's own smile became much bigger. Maddie could just about read his mind—*She likes me! She likes me!*

"You'd really do that for me?" Maddie asked him. She made sure to sound as sweet as sugar.

"Of course I would!"

Maddie moved closer to him. "That's so nice of you, Connor."

He blushed. Maddie couldn't believe it— he *actually* blushed. His cheeks flamed into a bright red. And his eyes shifted away from her for just a moment.

"I'm happy to do it," he said. "Do you want to start after school this Thursday?"

Maddie nodded. "That'd be great."

"And maybe we can walk to my house together, too?" He was as eager as a puppy when he asked this.

"I'd like that," Maddie told him.

Connor looked like he might explode with happiness.

"Okay, I'll see you then!" he said.

"See you," she replied. Then she walked away.

She didn't have to look back. She already knew he was watching her every step of the way.

This is going to be so easy, she thought.

Maddie sat in the greenhouse later that afternoon, going through her grandmother's book. She wasn't really paying close attention to the names of things. She was more interested in what they could *do*.

HELPS STOP COUGHING...

COOLS DOWN SUNBURN...

MAKES YOU SLEEPY...

Then she found a good one. It was

perfect for what she wanted to do.

She had just one of these plants. It was in a very large pot at the back of the greenhouse. There were lots of stems and dark green leaves. But Maddie was only interested in the flowers. They were a lovely shade of light purple with a bright yellow center.

She took out a pair of clippers. Then she snipped off one of the flowers. It was the biggest and most colorful of all of them. She placed it in a plastic bag. She was careful not to let the flower come too close to her nose. She held her breath to make sure she didn't smell it even a little.

She zipped the bag shut and went out.

Everyone filed into Mr. Crawford's

homeroom the next morning. Maddie took her seat in the back and pretended it was just another day. But she had already been here earlier.

Christie Walker sat in her usual place— middle row, third seat back. She was thin and tallish, with beautiful brown skin. Her hair was very dark with tiny, tight curls that stood straight up.

She went to put her backpack under her seat. That's when she realized something was already down there. It was a long white box. It also had a red ribbon and a bow.

She took the box out and set it on her desk. A look of tremendous confusion came over her.

"What's that?" asked the girl to her right. This was Amanda Belucci, one of Christie's best friends. She wore big glasses and kept her dirty blond hair back in a thick ponytail.

"I don't know," Christie said.

"Well, find out," Amanda told her.

Christie shrugged and took off the bow and ribbon. Then she carefully lifted the lid.

There were two things inside. One was the purple-and-yellow flower. The other was a small envelope with two words written on the front:

For You

Amanda leaned over so she could read this. "Ooo, how romantic!" she said.

Christie laughed, looking more confused than ever. "I guess…"

She opened the envelope and took out the little card that was inside. It read—

Christie,

A little gift for the new star of the play. Congratulations!

-Your Secret Admirer

Amanda's eyes opened wide. "Wow! Like...*wow*!"

Christie took the flower out and looked at it. "Yeah, wow."

"Do you have any idea who your secret admirer might be?"

"I really don't," Christie replied.

"I'll bet it's Caleb!" Amanda said. "He's *always* staring at you!"

Christie smiled. "Maybe."

"Or Josh Morgan! He's had a crush on you for, like, ever!"

Christie nodded. "Yeah, it could be him, too."

They went back and forth like this for a while. Amanda seemed like she planned to name every boy in the school. And the longer she went on, the angrier Maddie got.

*JUST…SHUT…UP…*she wanted to scream in Amanda's face…*AND…LET… CHRISTIE…SMELL…IT*!!!

Finally, after twirling it around in her fingers a few times, Christie did just this. She put the flower right up to her nose and took a big whiff.

"Ahhh…beautiful," she said.

It sure is, Maddie thought, fighting back a smile.

Connor's house was as neat and tidy as he was. The lawn out front was cut to perfection. And the windows didn't have a speck of dirt on them.

Inside was no different. Every room looked like it had been vacuumed within an inch of its life. All the furniture had a polished shine to it. And every little item had its own special place. It was the kind of house where you were afraid to touch anything.

Connor introduced Maddie to his mom. Maddie didn't think anyone could be as friendly as Connor. But his mom was so cheerful that she didn't even seem like a real person. Maddie couldn't even *imagine* being that happy.

Then they went into the living room. There was the usual couch and easy chair and giant TV. The walls were loaded with family photos hanging in frames. And all the shades were kept wide open, washing everything in sunlight.

"Okay," Connor said, standing in the middle of the carpet. "The first thing I'm going to talk about is *emotion*."

"Emotion," Maddie said, taking a seat on the couch. "Right."

"Yes, emotion. During your audition, you were reading Ruby's lines from that sheet of paper. And you read them just fine. But there wasn't a lot of *emotion* coming from you."

"Okay." Maddie nodded, doing her best to look interested. She wasn't, though. Not one tiny bit. "So…?"

"So you have to know what the character is feeling. You have to understand her inside." Connor pointed to his heart. "In *here*, where her emotions are coming from."

Maddie wanted to roll her eyes, but she didn't. "So what do I need to do?"

"Think about what the character is going through at that time. Think about what's happening in her life. Is she happy? Is she sad? Is she angry? Once you know, you can say the lines *with* those feelings."

"Hmm…" Maddie said. "I, umm…I think I get it."

"Well, let me give you an example." Connor went over to his schoolbag and pulled out a stack of papers. They had three staples along the left side. And on the cover in big letters:

THE DEMON CHILD

Right underneath that, it said:

OFFICIAL SCRIPT

Connor had already put sticky notes on some of the pages. He turned to one of them and said, "Okay, let's go over that same scene. The one with Ruby and her mom. Now, her mom is yelling at her right from the start. She's mad because Ruby has been doing all these nasty things to other kids. But Ruby doesn't care. All she says is, 'That's their problem, not mine.' Remember?"

Maddie took the sheet from Ms. Klein out of her backpack. "Sure, it's right here."

"Good. So, when you were up there, you kind of did it like this."

Connor read the line completely flat. He sounded more like a computer than a person.

And there was no expression on his face at all.

Maddie could feel a fresh wave of anger rising inside. There were few things she hated more than being told she was doing something wrong.

Connor seemed to realize this. "Maddie, I'm not, like, being mean or anything," he said. And that smile was back. "You should've seen how bad *I* was when I started. I might as well have been reading my lines through a phone!"

"So how do you want me to do it?"

"Well…you show *me*," Connor said. Then he shocked Maddie by holding out his hand.

He wants me to put my hand in his? Is he serious?!

"Come on," he told her, "I won't bite you."

Maddie knew she couldn't just sit there forever. So she put her hand in his—but only for a split second. Once she was up, she pulled it away.

Again, Connor didn't seem even a little bothered. "All right," he said. "Give it a shot." Then he stepped back, crossed his arms, and waited.

Maddie wished she was anywhere else in the world at that moment. She straightened herself up and cleared her throat. Then she said, "That's their problem, not mine."

It didn't come out as flat as the way Connor had read it. But it wasn't much better, either.

"Okay, that wasn't bad," Connor said. She could tell he didn't really mean it. And she was confused by this. If she were him, she would've said something very different. Something like, *Yeah, you know what? That was terrible.* She couldn't understand why he was being so nice about it. *What fun is that?* she wondered.

"Try it again," Connor went on. "But before you do, tell me—what is Ruby *feeling?*"

"Well, she's angry, too. Just like her mom."

"And she's how old?"

"Like, a teenager or something."

Connor nodded. "Right. You're a teenager, too. So how would *you* say this line to your mom?"

"Huh? Why is that important?"

"Maddie, a big part of acting is about using your *own* feelings. Finding the character inside *you*. Ruby is an angry teenager. And you know all about that."

"I guess I'd—wait a minute…" She looked straight at him. "What do you mean, 'I know all about that'?"

Connor laughed. "Don't be mad. I just… I see it in you. In school and stuff. You never seem very happy. I know what that's all about."

"*You?*" Maddie snapped back. "What do *you* know about being unhappy?!"

"I have a cousin, Jacob, who lives in Smithport. He's been through some bad stuff. His parents fought a lot before they got divorced. Then he and his mom had no money. They had to sell their house and move to this little apartment. Now he's angry at everything and everyone."

Maddie felt more of her own anger building up inside. *He's been watching me in school,* she realized. *And he knows about me. He KNOWS.* This made her want to scream. She didn't *want* anyone knowing her that well. Being on stage was one thing. That was pretending. She didn't care if people saw her pretending. But this…

this was something different. This was bad, and this was just *wrong*.

"...Maddie?" She heard someone saying. She looked up and saw Connor there. Then she realized she had gone off into some little trance.

"Maddie?"

"What?"

"Don't be mad at me, please? I'm just trying to help."

At that moment, Maddie felt something she'd never felt before. It was a warm feeling. A nice feeling. And she realized it was aimed at Connor.

You LIKE him, a voice told her. It came from far in the back of her mind. And just like the feeling itself, the voice was also new.

No! her 'normal' mind-voice cut in. *There is NO TIME for this*! *So STOP*!!!

"I'm not mad at you," Maddie said. "It's fine."

Connor let out a deep breath. "Okay, good. I thought you were going to be mad at me!" He pretended to wipe sweat off his forehead. "Whew! All right, so like I was saying, I think you should—"

His cell phone rang. He took the phone from his pocket and looked at the screen. Then his face crinkled with confusion.

"Sorry," he said to Maddie, holding up one finger. "Just give me a second."

He answered the call and wandered into the hallway.

Maddie couldn't hear his exact words. But she could tell he was surprised by what he was being told.

When he came back, he said, "You're never going to believe this."

"What?"

"Christie Walker isn't going to be playing Ruby."

It was almost impossible for Maddie to hold back a big smile of her own.

"She isn't? Why?"

"She's sick. Her throat has some kind of infection or something. She can't even *talk*!"

"Oh no," Maddie said. "That's a shame."

"It is. Poor Christie." Connor shook his head sadly.

"Yeah, poor Christie."

Then Connor suddenly brightened up again. "Wait a minute…" he said.

"What?"

His smile came back in full. "You know what this means?"

"What does it mean?"

"It means the part of Ruby is open

again!"

Maddie did her best to appear surprised. "Oh wow, that's *right*!"

Connor reached out for her hand again. This time Maddie let him take it.

"Maybe you can still get it!" he said, shaking her hand excitedly.

"I'll bet I could!" she replied. "If you'll help me some more!"

"Absolutely!" Connor told her.

"And if you'd maybe talk to Ms. Klein about it!"

Connor nodded. "I sure will!"

"Great! And then maybe we can be in the play *together*!"

"Yes! *YES*!!!" He looked again like he might blow apart from all the happiness. "Let's get back to work, Maddie! Let's make you the best actor the school has ever *seen*!"

"Sounds awesome!" she said. "Let's get started!"

That Saturday, Maddie was back in the greenhouse. She was wearing her overalls and her gloves. And there were smears of dirt all over them.

She had spent the morning in the garden. There were rotted fruits and vegetables to be thrown out. And there were dead leaves and stems and vines to be cut. She also did some watering and put down some fertilizer.

After all that, she went to the greenhouse for what she *really* wanted to do. She put on a cotton mask to cover her nose and mouth. Then she went to the plant with the purple-and-yellow flowers.

"There you are, my beautiful," she said to it. She wasn't even sure what it really was. It looked kind of like a daisy. But it also sort of looked like a lily. In the book, her grandmother called it a "Lovely Witch." Maddie looked this up on Google. But there was no information about it. Maddie wasn't surprised, though. Her mom once told her that her grandmother grew things that had never been grown before. And her mom said she didn't know how. She also didn't *want* to know how. She was just creeped out by it. But Maddie wasn't. She thought it was the coolest thing ever.

Maddie spent the next half hour giving special attention to the Lovely Witch. She carefully snipped off any dead leaves. She added fresh dirt with a little shovel. She watered it, and she gave it plant food. She also turned it so the other side could get a bit more sun.

Her phone rang. She pulled off her gloves and took it from her pocket. *It better not be Mom*, she thought. Maddie had told her a thousand times not to bother her when she was out here.

She saw on the screen that it was Connor. She gave him her number only after he promised never to call unless it was important.

"Hey," she said, trying her best to sound perky.

"Hey," he replied. He did *not*, however, sound perky in the least.

"What's wrong?"

"I just got a text from Ms. Klein."

Maddie felt her stomach drop. "Okay…"

"It said that Kaitie McKenna has the

part of Ruby now."

Maddie didn't say anything back for a moment. And that moment felt like hours. The volcano of anger that was always brewing inside her began to rumble. An eruption was coming, and it was going to be a big one.

Maddie hit the MUTE button on the phone. Then she closed her eyes and took a few deep breaths.

"I'm sorry, Maddie," Connor said.

Maddie hit MUTE again and took another breath. "It's no big deal," she told him. Pretending to sound like she meant this was hard. *Really* hard. Maybe the hardest thing she ever did in her life. Then she added, "I'm probably not ready for the part yet, anyway."

"That's a good way to look at it," Connor said. "I think we should keep practicing. Then you *will* be ready for the spring play. I just know it."

"I agree," she replied.

"Okay, excellent. I'll talk to you later, Maddie."

"Sure, talk to you then."

She put the phone back in her pocket. Then she closed her eyes again. She wanted to scream at that moment. Scream and punch and kick and claw. She wanted to destroy something, just rip it to pieces. There weren't too many things she hated more than not getting her way. Maybe there wasn't *anything* she hated more.

But that's not going to happen here, she thought. *Absolutely not.*

When she opened her eyes again, she saw the Lovely Witch there in front of her. She knew she couldn't use it again. That would make too many people wonder what was going on.

Then she looked at the book. It had solved so many problems for her before.

And it'll solve this one, too, she told herself.

She went over and opened it.

The following Tuesday, as Maddie was walking home from school, Connor called to her.

"Maddie! Hey!"

She turned and saw him running toward her. He was sweating and out of breath. But there was a big smile on his face.

"Hi, Connor," she said. "What's up?"

"Did you hear?"

"Hear what?"

"About Kaitie and Elizabeth?"

Maddie did her best to look honestly confused. "Kaitie and Eliz—no, what are you talking about?"

"They're both sick! Kaitie's got the flu or something. She has a fever, so she's not allowed in school for awhile. And Elizabeth broke out in some weird rash. She's been throwing up, too."

"That's terrible," Maddie replied. The urge to laugh out loud was very strong. But there'd be plenty of time for that later, she thought. For now, it was enough to be happy on the inside.

For Kaitie, she had used something her grandmother called "The Devil's Brew." It was an ugly plant with brown leaves and no flowers. The leaves had to be ground into a fine powder. Then Maddie sprinkled some in Kaitie's water bottle before gym class. And for Elizabeth, she used one called "Spider's Oil." The leaves were huge and shiny. When you snipped one off, oily stuff oozed out from where it had been cut. All Maddie had to do was rub some on the dial of Elizabeth's locker. Once Elizabeth touched it, the rash spread fast.

"It *is* terrible," Connor said. "But it also means you're back to being Ruby! You're the only one left who auditioned!"

Maddie's eyes opened wide. "Wow, that's *right*! Oh my goodness!"

"You need to get ready!" Connor told her.

"I know!"

"Lots more practice!" he said.

"I know!"

"Let's go see Ms. Klein tomorrow! I'll tell her I'm helping you!"

"That sounds great!"

"Excellent!" He grabbed her hand again.

And again, she let him.

Maddie spent all of that Wednesday feeling like she was the Queen of the World. She floated from class to class on a cloud of pure joy. She raised her hand to any question a teacher asked. And she smiled and talked with everybody.

Calista Harris even said, "Are you sure you're really Maddie Dragonette? Or are you just someone who looks like her?" Calista was in Maddie's science class. Maddie didn't really like her very much. But she laughed at what Calista said anyway. She was having one of the greatest days ever. There was nothing she loved as much as getting what she wanted.

After the last bell rang, she met Connor by the auditorium doors. He was so excited now that he hugged her. She didn't care. Nothing was going to bother her today. She even hugged him back, kind of.

They went inside and found Ms. Klein on the stage with a bunch of other kids. She was watching them build one of the sets. It was Ruby's bedroom. The character spent a lot of time here when she wasn't making everyone else miserable.

It's going to be ME in that room, Maddie thought. *Deciding who I'm going to be mean to next.* She was so thrilled she felt like she might jump out of her own skin. *And everyone is going to be watching…and clapping…and cheering…*

She thought about how perfectly everything turned out. Less than a week ago, there had been three girls ahead of her for the part. And her acting skills needed some work. (She didn't like to admit this. But if she could get better, then why not?) Now, all those problems had been fixed. Christie, Kaitie, and Elizabeth were all out of the way. And Connor was going to teach her how to act better than ever. Okay, she admitted, maybe she had done some dirty things. What she did to the girls certainly wasn't very nice. And letting Connor think she liked him...well, that wasn't nice, either. Not one bit. But...

But that's the way it goes, suckers, she thought. *Sometimes life stinks, doesn't it? Oh well, too bad...*

She and Connor walked down the aisle to the stage.

"Excuse me," Connor said. "Ms. Klein?"

Ms. Klein had some papers in her hand. They had sketches of what the set was supposed to look like. And there was a pencil between her teeth.

She turned, saw Connor, and sort of smiled around the pencil. "Oh, hi there!"

"Hi! I brought someone with me!"

Ms. Klein looked to Maddie then—and her face changed. The smile became a frown, and her eyes filled with a mix of worry and concern.

"I just wanted you to know," Connor went on, "that I'll be coaching Maddie. I'm going to teach her everything I learned during my acting classes. She's going to be a *great* Ruby!"

Maddie wanted to feel as excited as he did. And she had, a moment ago. But something wasn't right, she realized. Something was very much *not* right.

Ms. Klein took the pencil from her

mouth. "That's very nice of you, Connor," she said. "But the truth is, I'm going to be holding more auditions for the part."

Maddie felt every inch of her body frost over. Her brain struggled to absorb what she'd just heard. And all she could do was stare. Stare and wish all sorts of horrible things on this person she instantly hated.

"But…that's not fair," Connor said. He didn't raise his voice, but it was firm and strong. "*She* auditioned. I guess she wasn't as good as the others. But she's getting better! I'm already working with her to—"

Ms. Klein put a hand up. "I'm sure you are. And I'm sure she *is* getting better because of it. But she's just not…" Ms. Klein paused here to choose just the right words. "She's just not very good yet." Then she looked at Maddie directly. "I'm sorry, but that's how it has to be."

Maddie could feel herself shaking with rage. The thoughts traveling through her mind now were truly terrible. She imagined Ms. Klein lying on the ground. She imagined her in pain. And she imagined Ms. Klein begging for mercy.

Connor turned to her. "Maddie, I'm sorry. But remember, in the spring—"

Maddie spun around and began stomping up the aisle. Connor followed, calling her name over and over. She couldn't have cared less. She smacked the door open and continued into the hallway.

Then Connor appeared in front of her.

"Maddie, listen—" he said. He was walking backward to keep up with her.

"Get out of my way," she told him.

"No, Maddie. No! Just *listen*!"

He stopped, forcing her to stop, too. "We'll fix this!" he said. "We'll keep practicing until you're the best actor around! And when auditions for the spring play—"

"I don't care about the spring play. Or acting. Or anything."

"Oh, come on. I know how much you want to do this!"

"*Wanted* to," she said.

"I don't believe that," he replied.

"Believe it. Now get out of the way!" she commanded.

But he didn't. Instead, he put his hands on her shoulders. Their faces were very close now.

"Look, you have *got* to stop being like this. You can't just be angry all the time!"

"Don't tell me what I have to—"

"I saw what it did to my cousin! What it's

still doing to him!"

"Move, Connor."

"No! Not until you—"

Maddie pushed him aside. She didn't do it hard. Just enough to get him out of the way.

She reached the door that led outside and was gone.

Maddie didn't even bother going into the house to see her mom first. She went straight to the greenhouse. She was still trembling with fury.

She picked up the book and began flipping pages aside. Soon she was at the very back. There were a few things there she had never used before. She did grow these plants in the greenhouse. But she had never done anything with them.

She read through each one carefully. She wanted something very special for Ms. Klein. Something that would *really* hurt.

HAND OF THE DEMON...

WOLF'S EYES...

WHITE SHADOW...

Then she came across the perfect one:

BLOOD OF MIDNIGHT.

Yeah, she thought, *I remember this one.* She read what her grandmother wrote about what it would do to a person.

"Perfect," she said.

It was the ugliest thing in the whole greenhouse. The leaves were black and shriveled. And they were all tightly packed together. It didn't even look like it was alive.

But her grandmother had written about that, too. *It might look dead*, she'd said, *but it's not. It's almost impossible to kill one of these. That's because they're so nasty—and nasty things live the longest.*

Maddie tried to snip some of the leaves off with a pair of scissors. But they were too tough. Then she tried clippers. She had to squeeze the handles with all her might. Finally, she cut one free. It fell to the table like a dead fly. It didn't look like much, all curled up and wrinkled. But her grandmother had said just one leaf was more than enough.

Maddie got a little plastic baggie. It was the kind used to hold sandwiches. She held it open at the edge of the table. Then she pushed the leaf into the bag with a little shovel. She didn't want to touch it.

She put the baggie in her pocket and turned to go out. "Okay, Ms. Klein, get ready.

You're about to have a very bad day."

Then her phone rang. She pulled it quickly from her pocket, already knowing who it was. Sure enough, Connor's number was on the screen.

Forget it, she thought. *I've got more important things to do.*

But as soon as the ringing stopped, it started again. And again, and again. She hadn't even left the garden yet.

Finally, she hit the answer icon and shouted, "Leave me *alone*, Connor!"

"Maddie, you're in big trouble!" he said.

She stopped at the gate. "What?"

"Maddie, please tell me this isn't true!" He sounded very upset. More upset than she ever imagined he could.

"What are you talking about?" she asked. But waves of fear were already moving through her.

"Maddie…" Connor was breathing hard. "Ms. Klein thought it was strange that the other girls got sick. Christie, Kaitie, and Elizabeth. All the girls who wanted to play Ruby."

"Yeah, so?" She tried to sound like this was no big deal. But her voice was a little shaky. She couldn't control it.

"And when you got all mad before…that made her *really* think something was strange."

"So she can think whatever she wants," Maddie said. Her heart was pounding like a big drum in a parade.

"Well, she went to Principal Rosenbloom, and now…"

Maddie waited, but all she heard was Connor's heavy breathing.

"Now…what?" she asked.

"Maddie—" Now Connor sounded like he was about to cry. "Please tell me you had nothing to do with this. Please tell me that."

Now it was her turn to go quiet. She just waited, saying nothing.

"Maddie? Please tell me this is all just in Ms. Klein's imagination."

Maddie began to feel weird now. Not angry. Not scared. Just…*weird*. Like she was in a very odd dream, and the world around her was no longer real.

"What are they going to do, Connor?" she asked.

"They're—" He paused to sniffle. "They're coming to your house. I shouldn't tell you this, but they're coming to your house right now. And the police will be with them. Maddie, please! Please tell me—"

"I'll call you back," was all she said back

to him. Then she ended the call.

The phone started ringing again almost immediately.

She paid no attention to it.

Maddie went back to the greenhouse.

She stood there for a time, trying to figure out what to do. There was a small part of her that always thought this day would come. Sooner or later, someone would figure it out. She tried very hard to make sure that never happened. And now that it had, she was angrier than ever. But her anger was a faraway thing at the moment. It was like hearing music being played in another room.

Anger…

Rage…

Hatred…

These were the things she had always felt

most often. And she didn't just feel them. She *acted* on them. She let them come out, let them decide what she was doing to do. She thought back to all the things she had done in the past. All the mean things she'd done to other people. If someone made her the tiniest bit angry, she'd strike back. She never once stopped to think if the other person had *meant* to make her mad. Or if she really *should* be mad in the first place. She just felt it, then she ran with it.

Everything in the greenhouse was a part of all that. She had been growing these things to hurt people. To get even with them. To make herself feel better. To feel the joy of knowing she'd hurt them. Even now, the thought of it was exciting. She wasn't sorry. She'd *never* be sorry. Connor had been so wrong to think she could change. She didn't just carry the hate. She *loved* it.

"But you all have to go away now," she said out loud. It was like she was talking to a room full of children. "I'm sorry, but I have to get rid of you for awhile. So *I* don't get in trouble."

You'll be back, though, she vowed silently. *I'll get all of you growing again. And when I do, I'm going to get even with EVERYONE.*

She put her gloves back on. Then she grabbed the biggest pair of clippers she had. They were for trimming the bushes around the house. They looked like a giant X when they were fully open.

She went to the Blood of Midnight plant. She knew this would be a tough one. She took a deep breath and started hacking away. It took a few minutes to cut it all down. Then she went to the White Shadow. It had long shoots that went straight up. It was much easier to clear off than the Blood of Midnight. She stuffed both into a big garbage bag. She planned to throw the bag over the fence after it was full. No one would see it back there.

She was about to start chopping the Lovely Witch next. Then she felt a tap on her shoulder. Her first thought was, *How did Connor get in here without my hearing him?*

But when she turned around, she saw that it wasn't Connor. It was an enormous green leaf. It was curled back on its stem like a snake. Hundreds of others were there, too. Somehow, all the other plants in the greenhouse had grown super big, super fast.

Maddie's eyes widened, and she opened her mouth to scream. But one of the big leaves jammed itself in there before she could. Then the others went quickly to work. She could feel vines slithering around her arms and legs.

She tried to break free, but she had no chance. They were just too strong. And her screams were trapped inside of her. It sounded like there were a million bees living in her lungs.

The leaves continued growing at the same super-fast speed. They quickly covered every inch of her. Her face, which was bright with terror, was covered last. The Maddie-shaped pile of living green shook a few more times after that.

Then it stopped.

Connor arrived at Maddie's house with everyone else. He had zoomed over on his bicycle. The police went inside to speak with Maddie's mom. Ms. Klein and Principal Rosenbloom went with them.

Connor knew he wouldn't be allowed in. So he wandered around and waited. Then, through the fence on the eastern side, he thought he heard something. At first it sounded like the rustle of leaves. Like the sound they made when the wind blew them across the ground. Then he thought he heard a scream. He wasn't sure, because it wasn't a very *strong* sound. It was like someone screaming with a pillow over their face.

"Maddie?" he called out. The scream came again, but it was even weaker this time. Then it stopped altogether.

He climbed over the fence and into the garden. He looked all around but saw nothing. The smell of the fruits and vegetables was heavy in the air. So was all the soft, clean dirt.

He noticed the greenhouse and walked over to it. The door was wide open. When he stepped in, he saw all the plants and flowers. There were hundreds, on the tables and on the shelves. And they were all kept so neat and nice.

Then he saw the book. It was lying there, still open to one of the last pages. Connor leaned down and read that page. His mouth dropped open, and he could feel the sting of tears again.

"No…no, no, no, no…"

He turned back to other pages. With each one he read, another set of *no's* came out of his mouth.

When he set the book down again, the tears were streaking down his face. He understood everything now. Not just with Christie and Kaitie and Elizabeth. All of it. But rather than feel angry, he was filled with sadness. Sadness for all the terrible things Maddie had done. Sadness for all the trouble she would get into now. And sadness for what a nice girl she could have been. He just knew this somehow. He had *seen* it in her, although she could never see it in herself. If only she hadn't been so angry all the time.

He turned when he heard people coming. There was a whole crowd of them. Maddie's mom was in front, leading them to the garden gate. Then the police, then Principal Rosenbloom and Ms. Klein.

Connor turned away to wipe the tears off his face. Then he saw something lying on the floor of the greenhouse. It was gold and shiny. When he realized what it was, his heart skipped a beat.

Olivia's necklace.

He went over and picked it up. The flower pendant hung down from the chain. It spun lazily back and forth, catching the sunlight with each turn.

It was such a beautiful thing.

"Oh, Maddie…" he said softly.

Want to Keep Reading?

Turn the page for a sneak peek at
another book in the series.

ISBN: 9781538383629

The town of Kennisek held a flea market twice a year: once in the spring and once in the fall. To Brian Hart, it meant just one thing—*video game stuff*. No one around liked video games more than Brian. No one had a cooler collection. No one was better at playing them.

Brian and Elijah started at the first table. They looked over everything carefully. Then they went to the next table. Brian wanted to do it slowly. Elijah went along because that's what best friends did.

"Whoa," Brian said. "Hang on . . ."

The fourth table was mostly covered with junk. There were plates, dirty silverware, and an old toaster. But he saw a box tucked underneath. **"MISCELLANEOUS"** was written in marker across the front. There were all sorts of things inside: toy cars, pool balls, some broken jewelry, and a couple of Christmas ornaments.

Brian didn't really think there would be any video game stuff here. But he kept digging anyway. Two years ago, he'd found a Nintendo Game Boy at this very flea market. It was at the bottom of a box of old sheets and blankets. He realized then that he should always look. You just never knew. This time, though, he found nothing.

Halfway down the second row, Brian saw a PlayStation 4 with a bunch of games. *First released in 2013*, he thought. He didn't mind older games. But the salesman said he wouldn't take it back if it didn't work. Brian wasn't willing to chance it.

In the third row, he found an old Mario Kart poster. Mario Kart was one of his favorite games. He talked the seller down to three bucks. But by the time they reached the end of the last row, he'd found nothing else.

"One poster," he said. "One lousy poster. And I have to wait six months until the *next* flea market!"

"Maybe some of the car people will have stuff," Elijah said.

The car people were sellers who came too late to get a table. They sold things out of their cars instead. They were always in the back of the lot.

"I doubt it," Brian said, "but I'll check it out . . ."

Elijah said he was going to go back to a table they had passed. It had kitchen stuff and he wanted something for his mom. Brian nodded and walked away. He was still whining under his breath.

The first car person had a bunch of wooden signs. He had carved and painted them himself.

The second car had the biggest collection of sunglasses Brian had ever seen.

The next few spaces were empty. Then Brian came to the very last spot. An old station wagon was parked in the farthest corner of the lot. Its back door was open. The seller's table was covered with all sorts of computer junk—monitors, keyboards, cables, and disc drives. But it wasn't the computer stuff that caught Brian's attention. It was the person selling it.

ABOUT THE AUTHOR

Wil Mara has been an author for over 30 years and has more than 200 books to his credit. His work for children includes more than 150 educational titles for the school and library markets, and he has also ghostwritten five of the popular Boxcar Children mysteries. His 2013 thriller *Frame 232* reached the #1 spot in its category on Amazon and won the Lime Award for Excellence in Fiction. He is also an associate member of the NJASL, and an executive member of the Board of Directors for the New Jersey Center for the Book, an affiliate of the US Library of Congress. He lives with his family in New Jersey.

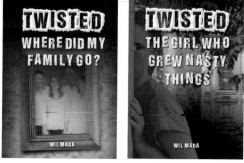

Check out more books at:

www.west44books.com

An imprint of Enslow Publishing

WEST **44** BOOKS™